DIARY OF A MAIL ORDER BRIDE

Diary Of A Mail Order Bride

Writer Sirron V. Kyles

Contributing Writer Irish Andrade

Table of Content

About The Author

Sirron V. Kyles was born in Texas and is best known as the creator of the Bob Marley Festival Tour, which laid the creative frame work for this book "*The Diary Of A Mail Order Bride*" as a Visual Communication Creative Specialist that focuses on Art Décor Corporate & Individual Branding, Photography, and Graphic Design.

His education consists of certificates from Rice University, Lee Jr. College, San Jose State, and degrees from Houston Community Colleges and the Columbia School of Broadcasting. According to Sirron, each platform helped him greatly with his writing and who he has become.

Honorably discharged from the US Navy, including three tours in Vietnam a member of the Special Services. A member of the High School ROTC and served on the Houston City Honor Guard, Color Guard, and Drill Team, which he feels was very important in helping him establish discipline early in his life.

Sirron played basketball in the Navy, high school, college, and professionally (mostly in the ABA).

Sirron has published several articles and other books that he either authored or co-authored.

About Irish Andrade

Irish Andrade, 30 from Cebu City, Philippines is a well-established creative writer, with over 10 years of experience creating valuable network ties with fellow writers.

Irish Andrade is an Energetic writer, who is skilled at focusing on finding solutions. Committed to producing quality work, she is a fearless artist willing to take creative risks and push through boundaries. A cultured writer, sports enthusiast, and savvy entrepreneur, with a deep understanding of the business side of the art of writing.

About Diary Of A Mail Order Bride

The presence of the First Lady Of The US, a former model like many of the applicants that apply to become a mail order bride has grown in popularity, "*Diary Of A Mail Order Bride*" Is about The Stories Of Two Mail Order Brides, that experienced Different outcomes.

In the twentieth century, mail order bride was a trend for women who live in developing countries seeking for a marital relationship with men from developed countries.

Originally, women from developing countries consider being a mail order bride as an efficient way to immigrate to a country with better economy, thus they can be exposed to more opportunities to change their overall life quality.

Chapter 1

Fashion Dreams

My name is Jenny Wu. I'm 24 and have just arrived in New York. New York - The Top 2019 global fashion capital of the world. I have dreamt of this since I was a little girl. I would do catwalks at home and strut around in my older sisters' dresses. They must be jealous now, all three of them, because I decided to marry for love. They say the eldest child is the rebel in the family, but in our family, the youngest gets her way. Life wasn't a big star-studded spectacle. I've had a few bumps along the way, but the man of my dreams, my knight in shining Versace amor, saved me.

His name is Karl Rossi. He's 41 but understands completely how the industry works. I feel like our souls met a long time ago and fell in love, and in every lifetime, we find each other and fall in love all over again.

I'm a second-generation Hong Kong immigrant. My parents moved here from Mainland, China, after their graduation. Like many traditional Chinese people, my parents got married very early. My mother was 17, and my father was 19. Their marriage was decided upon by their parents. Arranged marriage has been an age-old tradition in China. Unlike the rest of their family, my parents chose to engage in business in Hong Kong. In the mid-80s, it was very prosperous.

During that time, Hong Kong began to veer away from the manufacturing industry, which paid low wages that barely kept the population from going below the poverty line. The traditional Hong Kong people were fishermen. My father, a brilliant mind on his own, used what he learned in school and from his father's business, to start his own fish business in Hong Kong.

My parents' early life in Hong Kong was successful. My father was able to buy an apartment in Tsim Tsah Tsui, which was considered a very posh neighborhood at that time. My mother, who also held a business degree, helped with the business and kept his new house beautiful. They enjoyed five years together before the birth of their first daughter. My father was slightly disappointed because they wanted a son.

During that time, Mainland, Chinese men only wanted sons to carry on their last names and their legacy. However, he knew he and my mother were relatively young and could try for more children.

My mother was very hands-on with her children. She did everything for my sisters and me. When we were all too young for tutors which was afternoon cram school, she would teach us herself after regular school hours.

After two years, they had another daughter. My father became quite frustrated, and they tried for another child soon after. After their third daughter was born, my mother wanted to stop with three daughters, but my father threatened to leave her with all their daughters if they didn't try for one more. After having a fourth daughter, my father grew increasingly frustrated. He was getting ready to leave her with her four daughters, but my grandfather came to Hong Kong to intervene. My grandfather told him that while he was unlucky not to bear a son but daughters were a good investment.

The old man stared at his son. "Listen to me, Son. Educated daughters, who are obedient and loving, will bring bachelors from all over China, begging you for the girls' hand in marriage. Be patient. You will be able to choose from any man who come from a wealthy family and that man will help your business grow."

My father stared at my grandfather and I could tell he was thinking hard on what the older man said. Suddenly, my father seemed to have a change of heart and began to be more involved in our lives.

My parents were both strict with all of us. We could only wear dresses, had to tie our hair neatly with bows, study science and math, and learn to sing and dance, as well as keep a house clean. All three of my sisters were competitive. They all wanted to be the apple of my father's eyes.

From early on, it was engraved in our heads that we should be the best to marry a good man from a noble family. To my way of thinking, it was going to be our golden ticket from the hell our parents put us through.

My eldest sister excelled in math. From an early age, she could win math competitions, beating any school in the district. My second sister, who excelled in math, science, history, and the Chinese language, was an achiever. My third sister was slightly different. While she did well in school and kept her grades up, she was terrific in singing and dancing. She was our family's poster child. My father received invitations for her to sing on cable television and even an invitation to sing for significant Chinese events like National Day and other similar events. My mother was as busy as ever with her first three daughters, as they were all achievers. We followed her schedule to a Tee. She would ferry us around different tuition schools, and on the weekend when my third sister did her thing, my father would be involved in the ferrying around.

I felt neglected early one. I was the fourth child that wasn't special. My grades were very average, and I could not sing nor dance to save my life. As such, I received all of my sisters' hand me downs. I wore all their clothes when it didn't fit them, even their school uniforms. My lunchbox was from my older sister, who had some items broken. The Tupperware was from my second sister, and the water canteen was from the third one. Neither colors matched but it worked out. I resented my parents, but there was something that I was interested in.

Fashion.

While being the baby of the family and receiving all their second-hand clothes, I always picked my outfits and did my hair. I'd steal my mother's makeup when she was busy and stay in the mirror for hours until I looked like a clown. My mother was too tired to get angry with me so she'd be done after a slight spanking. It wasn't enough for me to stop. I'd play dress up for hours while my sisters were busy with their violin and piano lessons. This is where my love of fashion began.

As a pre-teen, I taught myself how to sew by hand. I'd read books about dressmaking and cut up old clothing that would no longer fit me to make new clothes. The most important part was that I didn't bother my mother and sisters, so they let me do my thing. Eventually, they'd let me make their clothes, and on my 10th birthday, my parents gave me a small sewing machine. It just made me love fashion even more.

While we were ferried around in a car to get to a lesson or shows my father had scheduled, I would sit quietly in the corner scheming a new dress or hat that would match a new outfit I made. When everyone went to sleep early at 8:30 on the dot every night, I'd sneak into the living room and watch Fashion TV until 2 or 3 a.m. The TV was on mute, but my imagination ran wild.

From then on, I would dream about becoming a fashion model. I was dead set on it. When I told my mother about it, she said it was only a phase, as she had a similar dream when she was young. She didn't understand. I was going to be a fashion model. I got my hands on every fashion magazine I could find. Our neighbor owned a beauty parlor, and she would give me all her old fashion magazines that were out of season. I'd go through each one and make drawings of outfits I was going to make.

Slowly, my sisters would come to me for fashion advice. I was the youngest, but I knew all the trends. I knew of all the Hong Kong celebrities and what they were wearing. I was my family's wild child, but that fact didn't sit well with my father.

He forced me to study harder in math and science. I'd make it enough to have above-average grades to get my father off my case. He'd follow up with me now and then looking at every paper, making sure I knew which ones I had made a mistake. He also enrolled me in piano and singing and dancing. I was into it for a while, but when the lesson was over, I'd be back to thinking about fashion.

My parents eventually decided that their energy was better spent polishing my golden sisters' talents rather than forcing the wild child into a specific mold, into something I wasn't, at least right then. One day, my father sat me down to talk.

"Child, me and your mother are doing all of this for you girls. Everything we do, we do for you. We are ensuring that our daughters get the best education. This way, my lovely daughters will have good choices in husbands. Young bachelors of good families in Hong Kong will offer their sons at our feet."

By the time I entered high school, my eldest sister was in her last year in university. My father started receiving packets in the mail from different Chinese families. They contained pictures of young men, most of them dorky looking, together with their college degrees and information about how wealthy their family was. It was like a Curriculum Vitae but for marriage. It was fantastic to learn about this Chinese tradition. While all my sisters ogled over the men and their dorky, nerdy faces, I turned the other cheek. No way would I want my parents to pick the man I was going to marry based on how traditionally Chinese he was. That was just plain crazy. I imagined myself as an esteemed fashion model whose face would appear in every magazine from Hong Kong to Milan, Paris, and as far as Europe. I would dream of walking the catwalk in Fashion Week in New York, and everyone would remember my name as this powerful woman who didn't need a man with her. The ideas became crazier and crazier as the date of choosing which guy my sister would marry came closer. How could my own flesh and blood allow our parents to bully us into marrying someone we barely knew? As a millennial in Hong Kong, the idea was crazy for me.

Chapter 2

The Obedient Child

"Obedience leads to true freedom. The more we obey revealed truth, the more we become liberated"

— James E. Faust

My oldest sister, Lisa, opened her graduation speech with this very inspiring quote. She is known as the obedient daughter or the perfect daughter.

Unbeknownst to many, my father was not happy with the birth of his first child. He had dreamt of the ideal son, a boy who would carry my father's lineage, especially at a time when my father ruled the fish business of Hong Kong.

In his mind, he had already planned out everything about his son. He even believed he would only have one son since the

Mainland had a one-child only policy. He wanted my mother to be focused solely on this son and raise him like the wonderful son they deserved. But lo and behold, their first child was a girl.

In a fit of rage, my father wanted to leave my mother because he thought she was the culprit in ruining their dream. It was the first time in my father's life that he was dealt with something he could not accept. With it, he snapped and wanted out of the marriage, not even thinking what would happen to a child he fathered. It was a good thing my grandfather, my father's father, came out to Hong Kong to try to iron things out. Since Hong Kong did not implement China's one-child only policy, he was convinced that they could have another child. It was also the first time that my father learned that it was wonderful to have a daughter.

'You just need to raise her well, and many will fall at your feet once she has finished her University," my grandfather had said, convincing my father.

With China's eccentric policy policing the number of children and the traditional Chinese culture of wanting male heirs, there was an unnerving disproportionate number of males than females in China. Families who had females could demand dowries and many extravagant items, so their families could merge with the marriage of their children. If you look at it, it was good to have a daughter. It took some time, but grandfather had eventually convinced my father that having daughters was beneficial.

According to the old ways, the obedient daughter was filled with rigorous discipline. My mother, who suffered tremendously and almost had a breakdown because my father was about to leave her with a newborn, raised her first daughter with a very disciplined and unforgiving approach. Imperfection was not tolerated. There was not a hair out of control in her very tight bun. She did ballet as a small child. She did classical music and poetry. She did everything our parents wanted her to do. She did not know anything in life. I believed that if my father and mother were to die before her, she would not know what to do in life.

My sister knew that someday, she would be married to the highest bidder. My father talked about it, as-a-matter of fact. It was the reason why all of his daughters had to work so hard. Lisa, from her earliest memories, had always been trying to gain our father's favor. He would tell her to make sure she would be first in her class, and she would not even sleep studying for exams making sure she was on top. She has dedicated her life to school. As a teenager, she had acne that stemmed from hormone problems because her body clock was so messed up. She persisted and always came out on top. She did well in academics and reasonably well in other aspects of education like sports, and even the singing and dancing part. She had friends but always abandoned them when our parents wanted her to do something.

My other sisters learned from her. She would diligently study and teach us at the same time. When either of us didn't get something right away, she'd pick up a wooden ruler and spank our hands hard. It was like a scene from an old Chinese movie where parents hit their kids, calling it tough love.

Whenever Lisa came out on top of her class or did something extraordinarily well and made Father proud, she always enjoyed it. She wouldn't do any chores and forced either of us to do it for her, saying that she made Mom and Dad proud, so she doesn't have to clean the house. When we became older, and the time to pick the right husband was coming, her bossiness went to a whole new level. She and my mother discussed the right qualities of her husband. She demanded that the potential husband's family pay a massive amount to ours. She wanted to have her own money as well on top of the dowry. She told my mother that is the price to pay for a perfect wife.

"Why would I be the perfect wife if I hated doing chores?" she said, as she rolled her eyes.

The thought still leaves me bewildered. But she was right. She was perfect in every way imaginable. I always boasted to other people about how amazing she was in her academics. She prepared her own portfolio to present to potential husbands. It included each photo she could find of any significant award she got, even going back to her primary school days. She added essays that were recognized worldwide, including one that was read aloud by the United Nations commissioner about children being the hope of the future.

When Lisa finally graduated from her University, she agreed to finally meet these men. She picked four from a long list of suitors. The four men were from the richest of Chinese families. Two of them were from Mainland China, one from Hong Kong, and the other was an immigrant family in Singapore.

She first met the one from Hong Long. He was 29 years old and a few years older than Lisa. He, too, seemed like a perfect match, but after going on three dinner dates with marriage in mind, Lisa decided to move on. She found out that while he was successful, he had a gambling vice. My sister didn't want to deal with that drama. Now that I think about it, going about marriage this way isn't so bad after all.

Should I just consider this age-old matchmaking process? I often wondered.

Lisa eventually decided on the man from Singapore. She decided she wanted to live in Singapore, which was as modern as Hong Kong, rather than go back to Mainland China in the smaller cities. She would be rich, but if she couldn't enjoy the lavishness of a city like Hong Kong or Singapore, what's the point? The groom's family decided to make a massive celebration in Singapore. They held a fancy wedding in Hong Kong but an extravagant and lavish one in their country. It meant that we had to ship some of our stuff to Singapore, as we'd need to stay there for at least a month. They agreed on the timing of their wedding, and lucky enough, I had 2 weeks off school to stay in Singapore and head home without my parents.

My life changed in Singapore.

The fashion scene was totally different than anything I could have imagined. While in Hong Kong, fashion was loud and a form of rebellious self-expression. Singapore was different. It had a more vogue approach to style and everything was high couture. All of A Sudden, the cutesy-cutesy outfits I would make out of old outfits meant nothing to me. This was new territory, and I was completely fascinated.

Our family invited some of our relatives to my sister's wedding and that was when I learned my Dad had a younger sister in Singapore. She was never mentioned in any of our family outings, and I found out why. She was the daughter of a house servant. My grandfather had an affair with a maid, and that relationship bore a daughter. My grandmother knew of the child but did not want to leave my grandfather.

Apparently, she did not want to leave her status as a legal wife as my grandfather was very wealthy. She paid off the maid and shipped her and her child off to Singapore. However, my grandfather was still in contact with the child. He believed that someday, she too would be an investment. She was given a good education and even carried our last name even as an illegitimate child. Eventually, she was married off to a wealthy businessman, and my grandfather did receive a dowry. However, the man left her for a younger woman. She's since divorced him and got married to a westerner. Her name was Cherry Mae, and I met her for the first time at my sister's wedding.

Cherry Mae was lovely. She told me about her life, married to a white man. She said it was the most liberating thing. I could see myself in her and could totally relate. I, too, was the youngest daughter and didn't have as much attention as I was nothing out of the ordinary. I believed my parents took good care of me to make me an investment, the same way Cherry Mae was.

She told me how much better her life was with her new husband. She told me how traditional Chinese methods are so outdated and that, as the youngest sister, I should consider marrying a non-Chinese. She told me how she could work by her husband and how she runs her own company in Singapore. They owned a small production company for fashion-related items. Although they were small and did not have a fancy client, it allowed her to express her creativity in fashion. Singapore was only a few hours away, but it turned my life around completely.

At the wedding reception, me and Cherry Mae had a moment when everyone else was busy.

"I made a white man and it's the most liberating thing!" she exclaimed.

My eyes grew wide. "Really? He doesn't try to tell you what to do?" I asked, bewildered.

Cherry Mae shook her head. "Of course not. My life is so much better with my new husband. He's nothing like my previous husband! Chinese methods are so outdated and let me tell you, sweetie, you should consider marrying a non-Chinese. I'm even allowed to work by my husband and run my own company!"

I was shocked. That's not how I was being raised and my dreams hit a new level. Was it possible? Could I have that as well?

She continued, a small smile on her face. "We own a small production company for fashion-related items and although we are small and don't have a fancy client, it allows me the chance to express my creativity in fashion."

Her words gave me a lot to think about. Singapore was only a few hours away, but it turned my life around completely.

And I knew I would never be the same again.

Jenny Wu

Photos By
Sirron V. Kyles

Chapter 3

Hard Work

— Jim Rohn

The moment I got home from Singapore after my two-week stay, I opened my laptop and googled: Modelling in Hong Kong. I was shown a slew of all kinds of advertisements for modeling courses. I wish I had done this earlier. I went through each link to see which of these courses I could afford with my measly savings. In one of them, the cheapest course I could find was HK$12,000 for a 1-month intensive course. A high schooler doesn't have that kind of money. However, I was off school for another 2 weeks. I could potentially work hard and earn that much.

I messaged my friend, who owns a small fashion-boutique in Sham Shui Po. They buy cheap ready-to-wear stuff from Taiwan and China and sell it at retail and wholesale prices. Without pause, she replied immediately, letting me know they do have a vacancy. The pay was a measly HK$25 an hour. I thought it was very minimal for such hard work, but if I were to get started on my dreams as a model, I would need all the money I could get. At that time, I didn't think I would get another gig who would be willing to pay me a full day's work for only the 2 weeks before school started, so I told my friend I agreed and showed up the next day.

It was my first experience with hard work. I thought I'd be in the boutique talking to customers about which cute tops to buy, but I was dead wrong. I found out that while talking to customers was indeed part of the job, I had to stock shelves and pack orders. The workday went by so fast that I could barely eat my lunch in peace. I'd be sitting behind the counter on a small stool with a lunch that I packed myself at 5 am, but when the bell rang because a customer came in, I had to swallow my food and stand up and attend to them. It was horrible. How could the working conditions of that store be legal? It made me realize that my parents are probably right. Marrying into a wealthy family might be a better option. I wonder if going in this direction, pursuing a dream that was so uncertain, was the right choice.

After 2 weeks of working, I finally got paid, but it couldn't cover half of the cost of a modeling workshop. Looking at the bright side, I think this is a good start for a fund. Along the way, I'd still be able to work some odd jobs, and knowing that I could absolutely do some hard work now, I'd even tell my Dad

I'd be willing to work at the fish factory. So, while daydreaming in class, I'd think of ways to make money after class. I'd have four hours of cram school, but then I'd have about enough time to work part-time after class. I wonder if I was going down the correct path. Yes, I'd make money, but this would affect my grades. How would my parents react to that?

It was a risk but one I was willing to take.

In PE class, Sunny approached me. . . She was a tall volleyball player. Standing at 5'11, she was the tallest kid in school. By this time, I was becoming a tall kid as well. I was already 5'8" by the time I was in high school. We had a conversation that would ultimately chance my path of direction.

"Are you working out during my two weeks off?" she asked.

I shook my head. "I'm stocking shelves in Brenda's shop in Sham Shui Po."

She nodded and we then proceeded to talk about how to earn money.

"I did some odd jobs growing up and started around 12-years-old because I was so tall."

Later, we found out that we both loved fashion. I was so excited about this newfound love I have, but what got my attention was that she was working as a runway model. Sure, it was small-time and for no-name brands, but I imagined it was a start. She said she'd make about HK$300 a day for a few hours for a fashion show in the mall, and she's never done any modeling course. She showed me a way to get in without having to break the bank. Could this be a sign?

I asked her if she could teach me how to walk the runway. She smiled and said that it came with a price. HK$300 a day. She said I could learn everything in 2 days as long as I worked hard. We set a date for training that weekend as I was convinced this could be it. She'd even loan me an outfit for the Casting Call. The Casting Call was next weekend, so I had to work hard. I could do this, and I was so excited.

That weekend, we met at an empty spot in the park. She bought books that I had to place on my head and heels higher than 4 inches. Wow, how could modeling be this difficult? The sun was getting hotter and hotter. My pale skin slowly roasting, and my underarms rained sweat. But Sunny was ruthless. She made me walk back and forth several times, try on several shoes that were difficult to walk in. By early afternoon, a tall guy came by. He kissed Sunny on the cheek and smiled at me.

Sunny introduced us. The guy's name was Vladimir. He was Russian, had blonde hair, and blue eyes. He was probably about 6'2", very tall and lanky. I could tell from the onset that this guy was one of Sunny's model friends.

"How do you think she's doing?" Sunny asked him. "Can you watch how she does, maybe give a few pointers as well?

He nodded. "Sure."

She turned to look at me and swirled her finger. "Do a little round on the makeshift catwalk we made."

Exhausted as I was, I went ahead with her play and found a delighted Vlad after strutting my stuff.

"Bravo! Bravo!" He exclaimed. "You might actually have a chance at the casting call. Would you be able to pose for some print ads?"

Print ads? Apparently, runways weren't the only bit I needed to prepare for. Vlad then led us to an abandoned building about 300 meters away from our spot at the park. He then set up some strobe lights and umbrellas along with a backdrop. Vlad wasn't only a model; he was also a photographer.

He held up a little bikini that made me want to flinch. "Go ahead and get into this two-piece bikini and I'll teach you how to pose."

He was charming about it.

We started to pose and take some shots when Sunny walked up to us with a sheepish smile. "I have somewhere to be and need to scram. I'll talk to you guys later!" she called as she took off.

I was feeling a little uneasy. Here I am with this white guy who I barely knew in a tight bikini. The comforting feeling suddenly changed into a bizarre vibe.

Chapter 4

Casting Call

I was incredibly scared out there when Sunny left. I didn't know
Vlad. Although from the onset, you'd know he was an artist of
sorts. He was such a perfectionist, and it didn't even feel awkward for him posing in sultry poses just to show me how it was
done. I felt scared but powered on. I'm in this already, and the
goal is to make it at the Casting Call.

Time went by quickly, and it was dark by the time we were
done. Five hours went by, and I didn't even notice it. Was I even

uncomfortable? He opened up his MacBook and made some quick edits.

"I'll need two days to finish these edits." With that, he turned and showed me some of the pictures he took. "They are magazine quality. Next time, I'll need pictures of you in the nude," he said, grinning.

My draw dropped open.

"Nude?!" I exclaimed, horrified.

He chuckled quietly. "Don't worry. You're a minor and need to be at least 18 to get permission to do nude shoots." His grin widened; his eyebrow raised. That alone further made me a tad uneasy.

"Pack up, babycakes!"

I knew what he meant. He wanted me to help him pack up all of his equipment.

"I have to get changed really quick. I can help when I'm done."

I slipped my top and jeans over my bikini. I didn't want to strip in that dirty place. I changed as quickly as possible, and when I turned around to help pack up, he was already done himself.

"You were too slow," he said, zipping up the last bag.

We walked together out of the old, abandoned building.

"How are you going to get home?"

"I brought my car with me," he replied, causing me to pause.

A foreigner with a car in Hong Kong means this guy is not one of those runaway models with a cheap contract.

"How long have you been in Hong Kong?"

"13 years. My mom works as a banker for the modeling agency during the casting call. I could move things around the way I want since the agency owes my mom a lot."

"Why are you helping me?" I ask him, confused.

"Money of course. I want 30% of your fees for every project that you get with the agency. I do like what I see so I'll hold off on getting a part of your money until you make it big."

I blushed.

I'm sure he's seen outstanding models, and that awkward photoshoot made it worse. But he assured me that he liked what he saw and that I'll go places. For some reason, it felt very reassuring to hear it from Vlad. I had just met him, and I was terrified to be left alone with him, but now my fears seem a little irrational. I think I should start trusting people a bit more now since I would be meeting more people from now on.

I walked back to the MRT station with a smile on my face. I am really looking forward to this casting call. This might be my big break. After getting out of the MRT station and walking towards home, it then dawned on me. There was more than getting picked at the casting call, a challenge that

I really didn't want to think about. They were the 2 people who pretty much liked to control my life, and they would be home in a few days. What do I say to them? Their last princess will not be presenting them a man from a catalog they handpicked. I can imagine the horror on my father's face and then my mother's heartbreak. She already experienced incredible heartbreak from my father, and she's been living her life trying to please him. With the way things are going, all of my other sisters will go the direction where my parents intend for them. I will be the only one going against it. How do I tell my parents about my decision? How do I ask them not to control my life? These thoughts clouded my vision as I walked home.

During the day of the casting call, I got up extra early and got a packet of food I pre-made the night before. I made up some excuse to my parents that we had a school activity that needed me to be there by 6 am. As all of my sisters were involved in after school curricular activities, getting out of the house at odd times was nothing new to my parents.

"Do you need a ride to school?" Lisa asked that morning.

I shook my head. "The trains are open. I'll be fine."

I took a shower, dried my hair, and applied moisturizer and lip gloss. Vlad and Sunny have said that many starting models make the mistake of coming to casting calls already entirely made up. The agents wanted to see the models' natural beauty, so I decided to be a plain jane that day.

By the time I arrived at their agency, there were already several people queued up even if the agency's doors were still closed. I got into the convenience store across the street to get changed into my little black dress and heels. I wanted to grab a drink but seeing all these stick-thin models lined up made me a little insecure, so I just skipped the option. I got back in line just as they were passing out the priority numbers. I was lucky number 62. I thought I arrived early, but there were a lot more hopefuls in line as well.

It was hot and humid, as always in Hong Kong that day. I was a little thankful that I didn't wear makeup for sure, everything would have melted off my face now. Slowly, small groups of 5 to 10 aspiring models were called into their office. Each of them hoping they'd be coming back next time for more opportunities ahead. There were a lot of western people lined up, and some unbelievably tall young people. When it was my turn to be called, I was called in the office together with 3 girls and 1 guy. We were all Asians, so there was no sore thumb that stood out. I considered that an advantage. They called my name, and I quickly wiped my face with a wet tissue to remove any excess sweat and look a little bit fresh.

"Do you have your portfolio?" one of the judges asked.

Nervous, sweating, I stepped forward and handed it over before taking a step back to wait.

I was fortunate in this department as I had significant help from Vlad. He gave me the pictures a few days before the event.

The judges all nodded as they flipped each page and that just made me more nervous. What were they thinking?

"Alright. We like what we see. Can you show us the rest of your stuff now?" said one of the western judges.

There were four of them in total. Two locals and two westerners.

"Sure, shall I start with the catwalk?" I asked.

The judge nodded. I was shaking nervously, but I kept it all in. This is my one shot, and I wasn't going to blow it. I got up on the stage and strutted my stuff the best that I could. I remembered every bit of Sunny's catwalk training and made sure I executed each pose to the best possible.

Then, one of the judges said, "alright, strike a pose," as he got up and walked towards me to pull out his phone from his pocket. "I want something sultry," he said.

I could feel my face turning red and my legs shaking, but I took it all in. After he was satisfied with the multiple poses he got from me, he went back to his seat and sat down. I also returned to my seat and waited for further announcements.

The judges then called each one of my companions and, one by one, thanked them for joining. After reaching the last person and sending him his way, I was the only one in our group who wasn't called. I was a nervous wreck inside. I could feel my knees and teeth chattering.

Suddenly, one of the judges said my name and I stood up.

"Can you do one more catwalk before going home?"

Despite trembling in fear, I nodded, taking everything in stride as I walked the catwalk once more.

Chapter 5

Mail Order Bride

All eyes were on me as I graced that catwalk one last time. I remembered all of what Sunny had taught me and all the sultry poses by Vlad. I believed that was my only chance to make it on my own before my parents could own my life completely. It was my last year in high school, and by the time I enter Uni, my parents will have an entire portfolio of guys to show me. I am the last daughter, so it will be their last chance to score it big. My father teases me that I am the prettiest daughter, and I do have that supermodel look, so I should go to the best family. It's as if I'm a prize for their years of hard work.

This catwalk is now or never. I did a little spin at the end and winked at one of the judges.

Let's hope I make it big here, I thought, my heart pounding with both fear and excitement.

They thanked me for that 2nd performance and asked everyone to exit the door. If we were picked, they'd call us back for a 2nd round of casting calls.

I honestly didn't expect a 2nd round. Sunny didn't mention that one. Before heading out, I went to the bathroom to get my shoes changed. I didn't have the energy to go home in heels. I was in and out quickly and then headed straight through the door, my pack thrown over my shoulder. I see more people coming in, so I had to make my way out as quietly as possible.

Suddenly, someone called my name and I paused, dead in my tracks. I slowly turn around. It was one of the production PAs. She was the one calling the candidates in and out of the building. She was wearing a blue shirt with black pants and had an earpiece on the left ear. She was sweating like crazy and looked too overworked.

"Jenny is it?" she asked.

"Yes," I answered, nodding.

"The judges would like for you to stay until the end. They'd like to speak with you today, so please stay."

"Did they say, why?" I asked, looking extremely puzzled.

She nodded; her sweaty head walked away.

Okay. Now my anxiety level is kicking up again. I walk towards the judges' room and wait outside. There was still a big group inside. I sat on the bench there and stared at the closed door. After a big sigh, a middle-aged man wearing work clothes approached me. He came from the door on the side adjacent to the studio.

"Are you Jenny?" he asked.

I nodded to confirm, and I felt as if my heart was slamming against my ribcage.

"Come this way, please."

I felt terrified but relieved at the same time. I thought I'd go home with my tail between my legs and my sister telling me not to be stupid anymore because I'll never be able to reach my dream. But was happening now. I made it this far. I invested this much. I am going to be a fashion model, no matter what.

The man leads me down the hallway behind the door. He walks up a flight of stairs at the end of the hallway. I followed him closely and saw the window open above the stairs. I looked out and saw the line go about three or four blocks long. How could I be picked among these many people? I continued to follow the man. He led me to the penthouse. It was an open floorplan, and there were a lot of people inside. Two women waved at me from what looks like the conference. The rooms were divided by glass so I could see them. They pointed to a chair across from them and I walked in, sitting down where they indicated.

"Jenny," The middle-aged western woman said. She sounded very professional. She was wearing a black tunic with black leggings and black heels that were about 4 inches long. Her hair was tied in a bun at the back of her head tightly and neatly. She wore cat-eye framed glasses and red lipstick.

"We'd be happy to offer you an in-house contract."

She placed the papers in front of me and got a pen from the pens lined up in front of her.

"The pay is not much, but you will receive full training, and we'll sign you up for some workshops."

I felt my heartbeat faster and faster. I could feel the color leaving my skin. I didn't know what that meant exactly, but it felt like fire. "But there is one concern…" she added as if she dangled the carrot in front of me. How could I refuse now?

"What would that be?" I said as calmly as I could.

"You'll need to quit school."

My heart stopped. The image of my mother and father flashed before me. Could I really do this? Could I break their hearts now? I mean…. I will be breaking their hearts anyway. Why not now?

My father would be fuming mad and slap my face. My mother, who had already suffered so much at my father's hands, would go through another heartbreak. Could I ask this of her?

Should I just put the nail on the coffin and come out as the Wu family's black sheep? Will all my three sisters come after me for being the only one who chased her dream and made it? Will they hate me for the rest of their lives? And more importantly, could I really make it as a model?

I cleared my throat and exhaled very profoundly. "Could…. Could I finish High School instead? I have two months left," My voice stuttered. My hands were ice cold.

She nodded. "Two months max is the best I can give you. Finish your High School, and when summer starts, you are leaving for Europe the day after."

Photo by Simon Bamidele Balogun

Chapter 6

Visa

Three weeks went by since I was given the contract at the casting call. I had five weeks left before school officially ended. I have kept it a deep secret from my family that I had accepted the contract. I have been walking on eggshells all this time. I had kept a secret that would surely upset them, but this was my dream, and I was determined to get there.

It doesn't help that all final exams are coming up. I wanted to give up since I am moving to Europe anyway, but this might be the last thing I do for my parents before all hell breaks loose. I hadn't slept in 2 days. I've been drinking too much red bull so I can study for the exams. I've also been asked to go to the agency a few days a week as well to prepare for my visa. I'm running on fumes right now. Once my exams are over, I can finally rest but my problems aren't over.

How do I tell my family that I am leaving in less than a month? I thought, agonizing over what I was coming.

My mother diligently helped me prepare for my university exam. I kept it a secret from my entire family. I would often make up an excuse whenever agency asked me to go to the agency to sign some papers. I'd be home late and then proceeded to study again. I can't give up my charade of making sure I do well on my finals. It was stressful. I barely had any sleep at all.

Two weeks later when I came home, I found my father sitting in the living room with my mother beside her. She was in tears while he was looking very angry. His face was red and lips tight. Both of my sisters were about 5 meters away at the dining table sitting with their books open. When I opened the screen door, they all looked at me as if I were a ghost that appeared out of nowhere.

My father stood up but before he could approach me, my mother ran towards me and screamed "Explain this!"

She threw a document package at me. I could barely catch it and dropped a couple of books. I stepped back twice and opened the envelope. I was surprised to see the visa documents for Europe. I had told the agency I need them to be delivered to the agency, so my parents don't see them, but I guess the cat's out of the bag now.

Explain! Explain! Explain this now!" my mother screamed, tears streaming down her pale face.

I glared at her, and then I looked at my father. He was just staring at me. Both of my sisters stood up but didn't come to help. My mother kept screaming and hitting me, but I could not feel any pain

Finally, I couldn't take it any longer. "Mom, stop!" I yelled.

Then, my mother started sobbing. She fell to the floor on her knees. Both my sisters then ran to her to try to get her to stand up. I started sobbing. I covered my face with my palm and looked down. I was so ashamed. How did this have to happen now? I prepared for this by making sure these would be sent to the agency. My father then called my name and asked me to step out of the house. He put on his house slippers by the door, and I followed him down the street. When we reached the corner, he stopped in his tracks.

"Why didn't you tell us you got a contract with that modeling agency?"

He didn't even bother looking at me. He lit a cigarette and continued. "Why?"

I sniffled a bit and said "You would have never allowed me to go."

"So you disrespect your father and mother by going anyway? Is this the daughter we tried so hard to raise?

"Please!" I begged him. "T-This is my dream. This is what I want to do. This is something that I worked hard for. You should be proud!"

My tears came fast as I tried to come towards him, but he took a step back away from me, glaring.

"Do you know who made you that way?" he asked.

"What do you mean?" I answered, confused. *What did he mean?*

"You are tall because I am tall. You are beautiful because your mother is beautiful. You used those traits that you got from us for foolishness."

I couldn't believe what he was saying. Of course, he was right but he couldn't claim credit for my being a model.

"But I worked hard for this! Anybody tall and beautiful can try but not everyone can make it as a model."

My father sighed "You are foolish!" he said, raising his voice. "Without us you are nothing. Do you think when we find a man for you to marry and a good family to marry into, it is for us? Of course not! Your mother and I only want to ensure you go into a nice Chinese family where family matters. We try our best, and yet you want to run away to Europe where no one will give a fuck about you?!"

"No!" I started answering back in a serious tone and was almost shouting "Dad, I know you mean well but I can't be like my other sisters. They live only to please you, but they're not happy. I want to do this. I want this for myself. I will make it. I promise you."

"Silence!" He shouted back. "No selfish daughter of mine will go to a country full of foreigners treating you like trash. You come from a noble family and yet you want to be treated like trash?"

"No!" I screamed.

"You go to your agency now and tell them you are not going through with this rash decision of yours. You will tell them you will cancel now, and we will go home together and tell your mother about this decision. You have one hour to do this or else you will no longer be my daughter."

He then turned back again and walked away without even looking at me.

Photography by
Simon Bamidele Balogun

Chapter 7

Find Me Someone I Can Marry

It has been two months since that fateful night my father asked me to cancel my contract with my agency. He gave me an ultimatum to do it that night. Instead of doing what my father demanded, I walked out with only the clothes on my back. I dared to do that because I had a little bit of savings, and I did more than enough to ensure I graduated high school without a problem. I couldn't tell my father to his face that I didn't want to fall into his money trap, so I left. I don't know if he waited for me that night. I don't know what happened to my mother, who broke down in tears upon learning I had my visa approved. I was always the rebel of the group.

Still, I know my mother was so busy with my 3 other sisters that I was the only one with the most freedom, as they often had no time for me, and I think my mother wept because she felt that it was her fault.

I am now in Paris, France. Part of my contract states that I will live here for at least 30 days before moving to either France or Italy. This place is different from Hong Kong. I imagined it would be glamorous like in the movies, but it's a complete disaster. The housing situation is terrible, and I must bunk with 7 other females in a room that's barely able to occupy all the bunk beds. The food is only great if you eat in restaurants, but I only do that once a week with a small allowance. I must be careful with my money. It isn't much, and it's all I got. I will be on my own after my 2-year contract, so I need to save up. I knew I couldn't go back to Hong Kong. It would be horrible to run into anyone of my classmates. They must all be in excellent universities when I get back. They'd be so intrigued why I didn't go to one.

I'm sure there must be some story out there that says I must have fallen pregnant, or they must have heard that my father disowned me. So, I have to make it. I don't want to return to Hong Kong. How do I get a permanent visa in Europe? But I don't want to be in any specific part of Europe. I want to be in Paris or Milan. These places are fashion capitals of the world, and I want to make it here. What must I do? These are the thoughts that keep me up at night before I go to sleep. It's not much of a resting place or sleeping place anyway because we are all cramped up in this small room. I don't talk to these ladies because they don't even speak English, but I did become close to one of them.

She was a Russian woman, and her name was Bianca. She was 23 and from a northern province of Russia. She had pursued her dream. , She didn't make it out of high school because she wanted to be independent as soon as she could. She was from an abusive family background. I could relate to her, but one thing about Bianca was that she was always busy on her phone late at night. She would escape from our small room and walk to the balcony, talking to someone on the phone a few times per night. After befriending Bianca and following her to the balcony a few days later, I found out that she had a fiancé. She was betrothed to an American man who lived in California. It must be great to know where you're going in the future and where you will be as a whole you be with, of course from your own choosing period none of that would have happened to me if I didn't come out here alone.

After a few fashion shoots together, Bianca and I became close.

I asked her how she met her fiancé, and she was a little hesitant to share the story. She thought it was embarrassing, but she chose her fiancé from a lineup of men. I was utterly astounded.

"What do you mean?" I asked her, confused. Did she do what my sisters had done? How was that possible?

"I was a mail order bride," Bianca said quietly. "I was told that American men have a high demand for young Russian women, and it wasn't hard to find one. I went through a couple of men but then I found Carl. He was the one for me. He just gets me," she finished, smiling.

She then told me about how Carl was in his mid-40s. He was married once before, but the woman cheated on him, and they divorced, and he got half of his money.

Bianca also told me that being a bride was simply a way for her to permanently stay in the US, but slowly, she was warming up to him. It didn't matter that he was older, but they were compatible in many ways. They found that out while they talked on the phone. She wanted someone who would listen to her and make her feel important and need her, not just some property that he would own. She told me he was active and likes to do things in nature, a companion if you may. Their story was fascinating, and in 2 more months, her Fiancé Visa would be finalized. She hasn't even met him, but they Facetime all the time.

"I know it sounds scary, but I've never been more sure of anything in my life. I know it sounds weird, but I've found my soulmate."

Her confession really rocked me as I stared at her, my eyes wide.

Perhaps I could become like her. I escaped my parents because I wanted to be my own me. I wanted to be the person I choose to be, and even the person I want to marry, and maybe select him from a catalog no less. Perhaps, I can find someone who has will be understanding and respect my choice to be a career woman and won't drag me down by forcing me to do housework. Perhaps this is where my future lies?

"Bianca." I said her name quietly but she heard me and looked up from her cellphone.

"Find me someone I can marry."

Photo by
Simon Bamidele Balogun

Chapter 8

How To: Mail Order Bride

"Adventure is out there."

Bianca's blue eyes lit up. "What?" She had to double-take.

"Find me someone to marry," I stated again, this time my voice firmer.

Contrary to what I was initially fated to do wherein my parents would pick the person I would marry, I can now do it myself, albeit it's slightly different from what I originally intended it. However, circumstance has pushed me here.

"I'm willing to try it. I have a few months to try it out because I don't want to go back to Hong Kong."

She laughed but once she knew I was serious, she became serious.

"Are you sure?"

I nodded. "Yes."

She nodded. "Okay. I was in a similar situation as you, so I understand." With that, she reached over and opened her laptop and soon had a website pulled up where I had to fill out the questionnaire.

I spent the entire evening filling out a very personal questionnaire about my personality and my expectations of joining the agency. I was terrified at first but knowing that I would have to go back home if this didn't work out was enough for me to pursue. I filled out the 15-page questionnaire and then submitted it via email. I received an automated response that I would hear back from one of their representatives after.

I waited three days to hear back, but nothing came. Bianca assured me that I would get a callback, but the initial wait was the scariest part. Am I really going to leave my future to something as uncertain as this? What if I don't like this man? What if I get in trouble with him? The irrational fears started to set in. Could I just eat up my pride and go home to my family and live in shame and eventually get married to a man they deem I am worthy of? These were the thoughts that kept me up at night.

My modeling career was going great. I have been approached by many smaller designers. I feel that I can go anywhere, but I think this agency might not be the right one. They seem smaller and work with many smaller designers. It's great for a start, but after my contract, I must try to go farther, or I might get washed away. Everything I learned here has led me to believe that I must set foot in America to make it in the fashion business.

And with that in mind, becoming a bride to an American is the fastest way to achieve that. I had some qualifications in mind if I say so. He must be unmarried; he must respect me as a woman and my dream vision and goals. He must not interfere with any funds that I will be earning for myself, and he must not demand children. I also thought about fulfilling my end of the bargain as a wife. Oh my. What do I know about that? Nothing. There is literally nothing that I know about that, so I hope whoever it is would be someone who would be more considering. I also thought about marrying an American model as a ruse, but online horror stories were too scary. I could get deported or accused of criminal activity. So, I guess this is my only ticket to freedom. I'm betting all my unhatched eggs in one basket.

Here goes nothing.

After about five days, I finally got the call I've been waiting for. It was a lady who had a familiar accent. After the familial boring questions, she told me that three gentlemen were interested in meeting me. She said I just need to give my email addresses, and we would start our correspondence with email. I agreed to the setup. An email was a great way to start the communication, so my pent-up anxiety won't spew all over the place.

Right before I could disconnect our call, I asked the caller the question uppermost on my mind.

"Are you from Hong Kong?"

"Actually, yes I am. I work with an agency based in Hong Kong." It hit hard. If this doesn't work out for me, this woman would be bringing me back to Hong Kong broken-hearted, literally.

Two nights later, I received an email from a man Joshua Cains. He sent almost like a resume with everything about his life, job, accomplishments, educational background, and even personal details like hid blood type and brief health history. It left me a little stunned. Do I need to know this much about this man? I haven't met him, but now I know him inside out. Does he have this kind of record of me too? In any case, I responded to Joshua's email with some intermediate attention. I should put more effort into this, I thought to myself.

However, he seems to be very dull and way too old for me. He is 67. I wonder if I could find someone who is not more than four decades older than me.

I also got an email from two other gentlemen. They were younger than Joshua but were equally dull or inappropriate. After exchanging a couple of emails, one of them insisted that I get on a plane ASAP to meet him. One by one these men were horrible. I wanted to call the Hong Kong lady back to tell her I wouldn't continue this as it doesn't seem to be what I imagined. I think I was about to give up after three months of emailing back and forth with these men.

Still, I received an email from an Italian American man. He was 37, which was not so bad compared to Joshua or the others. He was newly divorced but didn't have children yet.

"I don't want any children. That would take away time from my work, which I value. I want a woman who would respect that as well." I read the words again, unable to believe this was true. Could this really happen? He went on to say he lived in New York and owned an apartment in an upscale neighborhood.

However, it was his next words that really hooked me.

He owned a fashion Emporium

Photo by Simon Bamidele Balogun

Chapter 9

The Italian Man

His name was Giovani Romano, and he made a name for himself with the Romano Emporium. He was a first-generation Italian Immigrant. He worked as a leather artisan in Italy, but he fell in love and followed a woman who had an American dream.

In America, he fell in love with fashion and discovered he could design clothes. He built his empire together with his then-wife; however, she was too demanding of his time and demanded a divorce. However, in fairness to his first wife, they did go to America to realize a dream and build a family, but then Giovani went astray. He discovered his love for the fashion industry, and his then-wife only became further and further down the priority list. He was in the early stages of stardom when his wife divorced him and demanded more than half of his money in Alimony, saying it was her funds that got him into America, so she should be entitled to his small fortune. His life story was incredible.

Unlike me, he had the opportunity from the start and went for it and never looked back. I wish I could be as brave as he is. My family's dark cloud will rain on me for a very long time, and I don't know if I will be able to recover from it at all.

In his email, Giovani said he wasn't looking to build a family but only a companionship of sorts, and so he thought I was an excellent fit for him since I understood how the industry works. I responded to his initial email as honest as I could be. I told him I did think I was too young to go into a serious relationship, but I wanted the result of whatever it is to be a commitment. I wanted someone to understand that I am building a budding career and that while companionship is great, I wanted someone I could be an equal with and who would respect my decisions.

I wrote a long heartfelt letter that expressed my own feelings, and I could only hope he would not be bored out of his mind. I received a response right away, but it was to schedule a Facetime call. My heartbeat stopped for a minute. I've only been corresponding with these men through email, and at least one of them had demanded to see me in person, but Giovani was the first to suggest the use of technology. I'm all for it. I agreed to the time. 10 am PST. That would be midday for me.

I lay on my bed, looking at the ceiling. I wouldn't know how to talk to a man. Yes, I've had some boyfriends before, but this is an actual man who may be able to change my future. How do I conduct myself? I thought maybe I should dress up a little bit. I know it won't show, but I think I should put a bit more effort into these things. So, I brushed my hair and put on some light makeup. I also changed into a sexy top. If I'm going to reach for it, I might as well sell it. The minutes seem to go by fast. Waiting for a facetime call from someone I have never met seemed so scary. It was like I was applying for a job with a particular goal in mind.

With only 5 minutes left before he calls, I wanted to let go of any expectations, so I don't disappoint myself. Whatever the outcome is, I will accept it.

The phone rings, and I pick up right away. I was excited and yet nervous at the same time. The camera pops out, and I see him on the other line. We exchange pleasantries and talk about fundamental things.

To my surprise, talking to him was light and comfortable. It was like a pleasant breeze that I overlooked because I was overthinking. We didn't talk about the same things that I talked about with the other men I corresponded with.

Talking to Giovani was like talking to a friend.

"So how is your life as a fashion designer?" I asked eagerly, really wanting to know.

He spoke about the fashion industry in New York and how he started, and his plans. I spent an hour and a half listening to him, and I felt like my soul got connected to his. I just related to everything he said. I didn't notice, but now I am on my bed lying down and pouring the camera into my face while lying down. I got so comfortable just by talking to him that I got caught off guard.

He, too, was in his bedroom and dressed in his robes.

After talking about his life and plans, he asked about my plans. "So, what about you?" he asked. "What do you want to do beyond what you're doing now?"

I told him everything. I told him what I was doing in Europe, what my contract was about, which shows I was doing, which clothes I was wearing, and he seemed genuinely interested in everything. He even gave me some fashion tips.

While I found that odd because he was so effeminate, it also cemented his masculinity at the same time. This man was a real man who loved fashion, and he knew every bit of it like the back of his hand. We got so into it that my cellphone beeped, and I realized my battery was down to 14% from a full charge, and it was a total 4 hours later. I looked at the time in shock. "I need to talk a shower and will have to hang up soon," I said regretfully. "But I have really enjoyed talking to you."

"I've enjoyed talking to you as well. I think this is the most I've spent on the phone in years, he said, laughing. "I've never had a conversation about fashion the way we have. Heck, most people either praise me too much by kissing my ass or criticize me and treat me like garbage. I view the past few hours as a kind of therapy for me. You're my personal shrink and so easy to talk too! Can we talk again tomorrow?"

"Yes, I could like that very much," I said shyly.

I was really looking forward to Facetiming Giovani again tomorrow. It was a bright spot for me.

Diary Of A Mail Order Bride

Chapter 10

New York Bride

Love comes at the most unexpected times. I've been talking to Giovani for about six months now. We already have a routine for our Facetime calls. I feel like we're teenagers, giddy to get on a call and chat. We usually talk about how each other's work life is. I am always interested in the business of fashion, and he seems genuinely fascinated in my life as a model.

"You've been influencing my creations lately," he said one day.

"I have?" I was shocked and touched.

I saw him nod over Facetime and a smile lit his face. "I've been doing very well and living my life as positively as possible. Instead of partying, I really look forward to our talks."

I could understand that, but I had to be honest. "I still go out. Life here is hard. Sometimes, I just need to be around people who share the same struggles, you know?"

He nodded, smiling with understanding. "I get that. I see nothing wrong with what you are doing."

That relieved me.

I thought he might be turned off by my constant partying ways, but he said that my lifestyle is part of the business. Can you imagine how lucky I am? I have hit the jackpot.

I then decided to push my luck further and took a deep breath, almost afraid of his answer.

"What are your intentions towards me?"

I wanted to know early on as I am fighting against time, and although I really do enjoy my time with him, I want to know I can sleep at night wondering where I might be headed to after my contract expires. I was honest with him. It was the first time that I had ever cried out to someone about my problems. I thought I was strong enough, but I just needed this moment. I needed a shoulder to cry on, and this Italian Man was there.

There was a pause. "I'm serious about you. I would like you to join me in New York when your contract is up. I do want to take our time, but you can see how you fare in my lifestyle. And if you don't like it, I'll even pay to send you anywhere you want to go." He finished gently.

My heart was relieved. It felt like a huge block of ice that crushed me was lifted. I could breathe. I was thankful that he felt that way.

"Thank you. You have no idea how relieved I am to hear that," I told him.

We went on for hours on end. I could finally sleep at night, knowing I would be headed to Giovani. I have never met him personally, but I felt like I have known him all my life. He was the first one to understand me. I remember reading an excerpt about a certain religion that believed their fate was sealed and that they were just living according to the script, and nothing was done that wasn't written. It was all fate and predestined. Could it be that I had to endure everything that I did to be lead this way? My heart was full.

Weeks later, I prepared my paperwork for my visa. This time I didn't have to hide and be confused. Giovani hired an attorney who specialized in this service, and everything went very smoothly. I shared it with my housemates, and in my last week at the house, we had a big party. We celebrated how I found love, and this time I didn't object. I think I have grown to love Giovani. I say it without even knowing what it means. I am young, but I think I have been through much. My family all turned their backs on me, and I thought my world would end, but it was just beginning. Sure, I missed my mother at times. I missed my sisters too but achieving my dreams when I thought it was almost impossible made me so happy. Now, I am living the dream.

My visa arrived just in time, and I flew straight to the United States. Once my contract was up, the agency paid for my plane ticket home, but I had the tickets refunded, and Giovani was kind enough to send me a new one. He promised he'd pick me up at the airport too. I knew he was a busy man, but he was equally as excited as I was.

When my plane landed, the reality of what I was doing began sinking in. I was so nervous. I almost felt like using my own money to get a ticket to fly back to Hong Kong, but that ship had sailed, and now I was at JFK.

I passed Immigration and picked up my bag from the luggage carousel. I slowly made my way through the arrivals. I know his face from memory, but I wasn't sure if it would feel the same way in person. It didn't help that there were too many people too. My heartbeat grew faster and faster.

Until there he was. A middle-aged man who was thin and very well dressed. He was wearing a deep maroon suit because he just came from a business meeting. He was carrying a small cardboard frame with my name on it, and he had a bouquet of flowers and a teddy bear in his hand. He was wearing the sweetest smile from anyone at the airport. I knew then I was marrying this man.

Conclusion

It's been six years since I arrived at JFK on that fateful day. A lot has changed since then. First, Giovani and I got married two years after I arrived. We took our time. We almost didn't make it, but we eventually did. Giovani is more than a businessman now. We have a son who is almost two years old. He also created a new arm in his fashion empire and allowed me to lead it. It was one of his biggest business ventures, but he said he was never prouder of his new business partner, me. I didn't rely on Giovani's help. Together with a new marriage and a new child, I worked my way up to make sure his investment in me didn't go to waste. I now lead an equally successful business to Giovani's. He treats me as an equal and a partner, aside from being his wife too.

Last year on my birthday, Giovani surprised me by sending my parents to New York. It was the first time we got to talk in a long time, and when they saw I was happy and successful, they didn't care about their tradition. They were happy to see their new grandchild and me.

So, there is success in this non-conventional way of finding a husband just as there is success in fixed marriage arrangements. To each his own, and I am glad that I had gone through this route.

I wouldn't have it any other way.

Jenny's mail order bride experience, was not always the norm;

Diary Of A Mail Order Bride II,

as Peony's Diary story below will attest too had
a different out come.

Diary Of A Mail Order Wife

The Struggles & Happiness Of A Mail Order Wife

by
Sirron Kyles and Irish Andrade

Part 1

The Struggles (Rough childhood)

My name is Peony Chen. I turned 21 years old four months ago, and today, I am meeting the man I am marrying. His name is Christian Wells. He is an educated middle-aged man from Scotland. He says he is 41, but the photo he sent the agency didn't look like it. He has blonde hair and blue eyes. It's every Asian woman's dream to find such a man. Our circumstances might have been not so ideal, but we have been talking for a year through emails, phone calls, and on Whatsapp, so I am more comfortable now than when it first started.

Growing up, getting even the basics has always been a struggle, but both my mother and father managed to make ends meet. You see, our family of four live in a 300 square feet public rental housing flats in Kowloon Bay. The rent is Two Thousand Hong Kong Dollars a month. It's almost impossible to find housing this cheap, so we are lucky. My parents met when my father was on a business trip to mainland China in 1992. He was a construction worker in a small-time company, and my mother was selling cooked food for takeaways in a small canteen for employees. My father ended up staying in China for a long time, and after saving up some money, they moved to Hong Kong in 1999 and got married. I was born in the same year. I was their beautiful pride and joy. My father named me Peony after the lovely flowers he took care of when he worked as a gardener for a big financial firm in Hong Kong. While they reveled in their joy on the birth of their daughter, the money that they saved for their big move didn't last. My mother went back to work a few months after my birth.

My childhood was neglectful. My parents were always busy working, and I had to learn to ride the train to my kindergarten at six years old. That was not uncommon. Many poverty-stricken and middle-income families' children did the same, so I did not know that this was out of the ordinary.

When I started primary school, my mother had an unplanned pregnancy. My dad often stayed home when he got laid off his construction job. They decided they wanted an abortion as it was too challenging to take care of two children given my father's unstable jobs. However, everything changed when they learned that my mother was pregnant with a boy.

They had longed for a boy. A boy often meant fulfillment for the typical Chinese family. My father had to accept several menial jobs like restaurant delivery and cleaning street alleys. My parents were overwhelmed with joy when my brother was born. It made me a little jealous because it seems as though they were fed up with life when I was their only daughter, but now with a boy, everything had meaning. Would they have traded me for a boy then? Who knows.

Life took a turn when their precious little boy turned two. He was different from other children and often screamed non-stop for hours on end. Our landlord often knocked on our door, demanding we keep the child quiet as he was disturbing our neighbors. Later on, my brother was diagnosed with severe autism. It explained his bouts of rage that were more than just flaring temper tantrums. Not long after the diagnosis was confirmed, we got kicked out of that flat.

My parents' dreams started to fall apart, and they were back to the neglectful parents they were. At an early age, I learned to restrain my brother using my hands and a makeshift rag that I would use to muffle the sound of his constant screaming. My mother worked during the day and my father at night so they could take turns in taking care of us. I had to run to school and run back, making sure that my brother didn't ruin the day enough so my father would have enough sleep to go on his night shift.

Despite how difficult life was, it had worked. It was like a well-oiled machine that functioned adequately as long as we all did our parts, but that rickety machine broke down as soon as I finished my Secondary school. My mother had a stroke and became partially paralyzed. My father then had to work morning and evening. In an instant, my hard work in passing the Hong Kong Diploma of Secondary Education (HKDSE) was thrown away. I could no longer afford to go to college.

Am I doomed to the mediocre life that my parents have?
Or is there a way out of this for me? These were
the questions I asked myself daily, and the answers
looked scarier with each passing day.

Part 2

The Struggles (Growing up)

Am I doomed to the mediocre life that my parents have? Or is there a way out of this for me? These were the questions I asked myself daily, and the answers looked scarier with each passing day.

It's been two years since I had to stop school because my couldn't afford to pay for my college fees. My mother has gotten a little better-well enough to take care of herself and my brother. I had also started doing some part-time jobs, but my meager income of HK$1,000 per month was not enough to help out. To be a young woman living in the bitterness of being poor in a glamorous city makes me cry every day.

Seven months ago, when the protests against the CCP started ravaging Hong Kong, my father lost his construction job, which held us together. We both had to work odd jobs just to get food on our table. Last month, the electric company cut off our power. Going home every day became miserable. At the same time, my former boss, the older man who ran the restaurant where I worked as a waitress three years ago contacted me and called me to come to the shop. He was amiable and gave me some money and food that would last us a week. I knew I could pay our neighbor a few dollars to let us store the food in their fridge, but his intention became more evident after I accepted his donations. He introduced his son. He was 29 years old and worked as an electrician in a computer shop Downtown. His father negotiated with me that if I agreed to marry his son and bear him a child, my family would get an allowance of HKD$20,000 per month. He smiled and got off the table. He said he would give me some time to think about it. But he left the fat cheque in front of me.

Without even thinking about it, I said yes to the arrangement. He gave me the cheque, and I cashed it the next morning. I turned our lights back on, brought a fridge, and did some groceries. The money left over would probably last my family for two weeks, and my father promised he would continue his odd jobs as well.

When I told my parents of our situation, they didn't even bat an eye. It was as if they had known that such a horrible offer would come my way and I'd accept it. I knew my life was going to be miserable, and I would be indebted to this family forever, but I just hoped it would find me a way out of this hell hole. I packed my bags and left our small room to move into this man's apartment. He lived in an apartment which he subleased. The living conditions were only somewhat better than what we had. He was extraordinarily disorganized and dirty but seemed decent enough. He said he was against the idea of an arranged marriage with me, but when he found out about our situation, he reluctantly agreed. Thanks? Do I owe him now? Things were okay between us at first, but whenever he got paid at his job, he would disappear for days. I later learned that he had a gambling problem. His father eventually confessed that he had no hope for this son and that he only wanted to marry him off to know that there would be a woman who would take care of him, which I did diligently.

On the off chance that he would make his way home from drinking and gambling all night, he would demand sex, and I readily gave this to him. I did not want to upset either of the new men in my new life. And when my husband got all that he wanted, he would lie in bed passed out. I took this time to search his wallets and take out all the cash I could find and hide them in my little stash. This was my new life. It went on for about a year until Sonia Leung came into my life.

Sonia Leung was a regular at our restaurant. She always came with a new lady every week. They were very young and attractive. Sonia was a middle-aged woman who liked to dress too immature for her age. She arrived 10 minutes to closing time one night and ordered a meal for herself. She was talking to a western man on a video call. She always smiled and seemed genuinely happy. When she finished her phone call, I took the chit to her, and she paid her tab. I asked her if that was her husband. She confirmed it was. I commented about how nice it would be to have a western husband. She stopped and looked me dead in the eye. I was a little anxious I might have said something I shouldn't have. I immediately looked down and hurriedly brought the dirty dishes over to the kitchen. She lit a cigarette and walked out of the restaurant, and I thought that was the end of it.

After finishing up for the night and closing up the restaurant, I stopped by the 7eleven outside to buy a drink. Sonia was waiting for me outside, still with a cigarette in her right hand. "Do you want a western husband?" she asked....

What would Peony Chen's answer to this question be
and what difference would it make. Could this be
the answer that would change her life forever?

Part 3

Finding Happiness

After finishing up for the night and closing up the restaurant, I stopped by the 7eleven outside to buy a drink. Sonia was waiting for me outside, still with a cigarette on her right hand. "Do you want a western husband?" she asked.

She had a slight grin and seemed delighted to ask me. I felt a little cornered. I told her that I would be married soon. I was living with my husband already. We just haven't found time for the ceremony. She nodded her head as if she agreed. She pulled me to the McDonald's beside the convenience store and told me about her life as an agent HKBeauties.com. A quick Google search will tell you that it's a Mail Order Bride Service.

Mail Order Brides are not uncommon. I know of a few of my mother's relatives from mainland China who were sent off somewhere with an older white gentleman, most of them against their will. But Sonia Leung was not one of them. She told me how happy she is with her life now. She explained how she was married to a businessman who was away every month for business but eventually left her for a younger woman. She told me how much she wallowed in pain every night until her kids were old enough to leave their home. Then, she considered becoming a Mail Order Bride. Who knew a middle-aged woman could still become a Mail Order Bride. I didn't, but Sonia proved me wrong.

She went into detail about the process: Submit your personal information to the company, the company does a background check, and then they take new photos to be sent to their counterpart in the west. It would be like a modeling portfolio, but you are applying to become a wife. She then told me that if a man were to become serious with me, he would be willing to bail me out of my current situation and pay to get me to his country. This idea scared me.

What if this man, whom I had never met but agreed to marry, would kill me while sleep? I let Sonia know of my fears and she assured me that my fears were very valid and that her counterpart also did the same kind of vetting they would do to me if I agreed. At this point, I was convinced.

Western men seemed more affectionate towards their women, and they have a level of respect that many Chinese men don't. I explained to Sonia that if there were such a man who would be willing to put me out of my misery in my loveless pretend marriage, I would agree to marry him. Sonia agreed. She asked for my email address so she could send some e-forms later. It was after midnight when we parted. True to her word, when I woke up, Sonia had sent some forms. They were very long and extremely specific. They required my blood type, the name of all my doctor's, and all sorts of stuff. I filled out the entire form hoping that my investment of 40 minutes will lead me to a life where I could be happy forever. I spilled my heart and soul on that form. I wanted all that Sonia promised me.

Two weeks had passed when I received another message from Sonia. She asked if I could come to a particular Photo Studio somewhere in Central. "It will take at least four hours," She said in her SMS. Without stopping to think, I told my father-in-law that I couldn't come to the shop tomorrow as I have an appointment for my annual medical exam. He didn't even question it. The Photo shoot was intensive. It was an hour's worth of my time getting into business attire, Sunday Dresses, and underwear. I was timid at first, but there was absolutely nothing provocative or lewd about this Photo shoot. It was very matter-of-factually done very quickly. I was in and out very quickly. When I was finally finished, I met Sonia outside the studio. She made me sign some waivers saying that I was authorizing them to give my photos to her counterpart in the west. She then told me that she would send me some emails from the men who would be interested in me. I complied with her request, and she sent me my way.

*With the photo sent, there was only one thing left to do,
wait. How long will Peony have to wait and will any man
find her attractive enough to bail her out of her misery?*

Part 4

Happiness At Last

She made me sign some waivers saying that I was authorizing them to give my photos to her counterpart in the west. She then told me that she would send me some emails from the men who would be interested in me. I complied with her request, and she sent me my way

Two weeks later I received an email from an Emmett Hansen. The email contained several attachments of Men's profiles. These were the men Sonia told me about, and I was happy to receive them. I haven't even seen the photos they took of me, but these men did, and they liked what they saw. The thought made me giggle. The Mail Order Bride Industry is real, after all. You only realize how real everything is when you get to this stage. Out of the men that sent me their profiles, I had eyes on two men: Brian Keller and Christian Wells. I sent both of them emails. It was amicable. Nothing too personal or scary. Brian immediately responded the next day, while Christian responded a few days later.

My conversations with both men were very different. Brian was aggressive and pushy. He wanted things to be arranged quickly. He wanted me to run away from my family, and he'll send me a ticket to his country. Of course, things wouldn't work that way. There were problems with Visas and of course, my family. They relied on me for everything. There was also the problem of my husband's family whom I am indebted to. I decided to stop responding to Brian after three months of correspondence. It felt weird. We even had a fight over the phone. It felt like I had a boyfriend. Brian then decided to harass me through an email saying he already invested in me and was going to ship me off to where he was. His emails become incessantly annoying, so I told Sonia. She must have done something because Brian's emails stopped immediately.

I continued my conversation with Christian. He was more insightful and cheery. He wanted to learn more about who I was as a woman. He asked about my childhood and I told him everything except the part where I was an unofficial wife of a man I was betrothed to. He was never forward in his thinking. He made it clear that he intended to get to know me to see if we would make a good couple and not to know if I would be a good wife. He was a true gentleman. On my birthday nine months after we started emailing every day, he sent me flowers. I gave him my parents' address so my current family wouldn't find out.

Along with the flowers was a simple note that said: "I love your company" and a small gold chain bracelet. It was the most romantic thing anyone has ever done for me. I'll never forget it. I then decided that I didn't want to fool Christian as he was too sweet for me. I told him the truth and was prepared for the worst. Surprisingly, he took it in good stride. He asked me what should be done if I wanted to get out of my situation. I told him there is nothing that he can do. I would have to slowly pay off my debt to this family and settle my family who is relying on me. Days turned in to weeks and months to a year, and we've been talking for an entire year now. He sent me a message that he'd be coming to see me a week before the Chinese New Year. I told him that we'd have to arrange to meet privately because of my situation. He then told me not to worry about it. Not to worry? How would that work out?

Three days before I was supposed to meet Christian, I saw Sonia standing outside our restaurant talking to my father-in-law. She slipped him a brown paper bag, and he hurriedly kept it in his pocket under his apron. She then walked away quietly. I didn't say hello for fear that my father-in-law would find out my shenanigans. I greeted him good morning, but he told me to stop with the pretend play. He found out about what I was doing and my intentions to marry a western man, and he agrees. Christian paid him off the value of his restaurant and the money he gave me to my parents. He told me I was free and that I no longer needed to take care of his irresponsible son. With the amount he got from Christian, he would be happy to look for another unlucky lass to take my place. I didn't want to smile, but the relief must have shone brightly on my face. I went home to my family right after. There, I saw Sonia talking to my father. My father greeted me and hugged me. He told me that Christian gave them some money too and he gave him a job with a good company. The money was not much, but he secured my mother's health needs and my brother's therapy needs as well. He also found a decent apartment for all of them.

In one click, all of my problems were resolved. How lucky can a woman get? Christian then told me he would be staying at the four seasons and that's where he would like us to meet. He booked two suites for us and asked me to stay there ahead of his arrival. After years of an endless battle with poverty, I found a way out. And as I sit here in this fancy hotel room waiting for Christian, I am happy to share with you my successful Mail Order Bride Story. It may not be suitable for all, and you may not find your perfect man right away, but always keep an open mind because that's the only way you'll know if it's right for you.

www.ingramcontent.com/pod-product-compliance
Lightning Source LLC
Chambersburg PA
CBHW061106100726
47911CB00012B/429